For my sublime sister, Josie, who is neither Mirabelle
nor Meg, but maybe a little bit of both
K. H.

For my beautiful Liliana, who has proved herself fearless
on many occasions, except when faced with a spider
N. A.

First U.S. edition 2019

Library of Congress Catalog Card Number pending
ISBN 978-1-5362-0811-5

19 20 21 22 23 24 TLF 10 9 8 7 6 5 4 3 2 1

Printed in Dongguan, Guangdong, China

This book was typeset in Caslon Manuscript, Circus, and Duality.
The illustrations were created digitally.

TEMPLAR BOOKS

an imprint of
Candlewick Press
99 Dover Street
Somerville, Massachusetts 02144
www.candlewick.com

FEARLESS MIRABELLE & MEG

Katie Haworth

illustrated by Nila Aye

templar books

an imprint of Candlewick Press

Mirabelle and Meg Moffat are twins,
and they **look** just the same.

But they are not.

Even when they were babies, they were very different.

Mirabelle liked balancing . . .

climbing . . .   and jumping!

"Mirabelle is so brave!" cried their mother.
"And daring!" cried their father.
(The twins' parents are famous circus acrobats, so this pleased them very much.)

Meanwhile, Meg just made
a whole lot of NOISE.

Goo goo!

He he he!

Goo goo!

Gaa gaa!

Goooo!

Gaa gaa!

As Mirabelle and Meg got older,
Mirabelle
balanced **higher** . . .

climbed **farther** . . .

and jumped from **greater heights.**

Mirabelle is so fearless!

And daring!

While Meg never stopped talking.

In fact, Meg didn't try to climb anything at all.
Not even the furniture.

One day, Mr. and Mrs. Moffat took Mirabelle and Meg to work.

In the circus tent, the twins' mother practiced
a triple somersault without dropping a cherry pie.
Their father leaped from a great height
into a pool of water.

Mirabelle was next. She did a backflip, leaped
through six flaming hoops, and cartwheeled across
a tightrope seventeen times.

Then it was Meg's turn.

And suddenly, for the first time in her life,
Meg didn't say **anything.** Her legs wobbled like jellyfish.
Her hands shook like earthquakes.

And Mr. and Mrs. Moffat realized . . .

Meg was afraid of heights!

Once they'd helped her down, her parents said,
"Don't worry, darling. There are lots of other
amazing things you can do."

Meg tried all sorts of things:

juggling . . .

horseback riding . . .

and playing in the band . . .

Wh_Aa WhuMp!

but nothing was right.

Meg shut herself in the family's caravan
and wouldn't talk to anyone.

Not even Mirabelle.

She wouldn't even come out to see
Mirabelle's grand debut. But the show had to go on. . . .

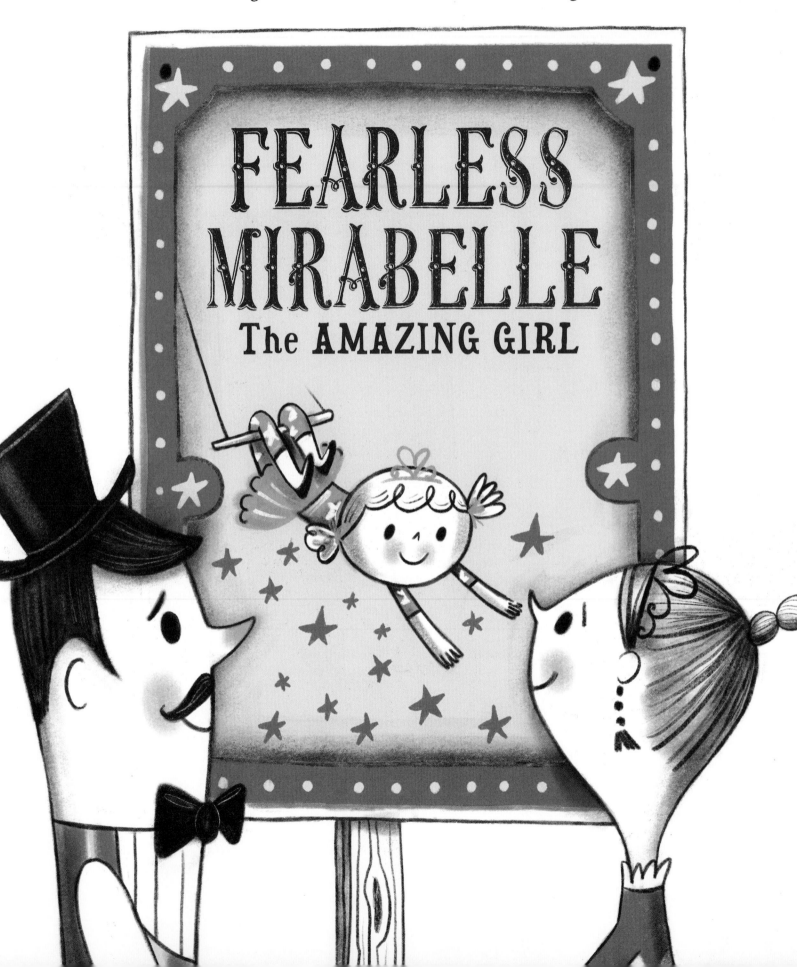

FEARLESS
MIRABELLE
The AMAZING GIRL

The crowd gasped as Mirabelle rode a unicycle on a tightrope.

They oohed and aahed as she jumped off and somersaulted down...

down....

and down.

They ROARED as she balanced on a galloping horse
and ate a bowl of cereal without spilling a drop of milk.

The show was a huge success!
The crowd babbled, cameras flashed, and microphones
were thrust in Mirabelle's face.

There was a great hush
as her fans waited . . . and waited . . .
and waited. . . .

Mirabelle's legs wobbled
like jellyfish.
Her hands shook
like earthquakes.
She couldn't say
anything at all.

FEARLESS
MIRABELLE
WAS

Just then, she felt a small hand holding her own
and heard a big, strong voice beside her.

This is my

AMAZING
sister,
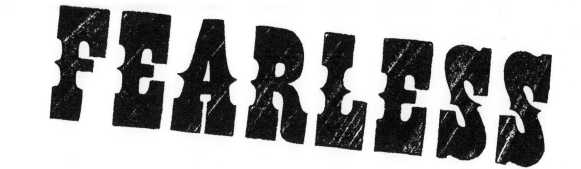
FEARLESS

MIRABELLE!

And from then on, while Mirabelle **fearlessly** climbed higher and **higher...**

Meg **fearlessly** spoke to the crowd.

Look at her balancing on the high wire!

Watch
her
dive!

See her swoop!

The audience leaped to their feet and cheered with delight.

The Moffats changed the poster, and the show went on.

So, although Mirabelle and Meg Moffat are
twins and **look** just the same . . .

they are not.
But they are both brave!